WHAT DOES THE FOX SAY?

'The Fox (What Does the Fox Say?)'
Lyrics by Bård Ylvisåker, Vegard Ylvisåker and Christian Løchstøer

SIMON AND SCHUSTER
First published in Great Britain in 2013 by Simon and Schuster UK Ltd
1st Floor, 222 Gray's Inn Road, London WC1X 8HB
A CBS Company

'The Fox'
Words and music by Bård Ylvisåker, Vegard Ylvisåker, Tor Hermansen,
Mikkel Eriksen, Nicholas Boundy and Christian Løchstøer
©2013 reproduced by permission of
Stellar Songs Ltd/EMI Music Publishing Ltd, London, W1F 9LD
Illustrations by Svein Nyhus
Originally published in Norwegian in 2013 as Hva sier reven?
The right of Bård Ylvisåker, Vegard Ylvisåker, Tor Hermansen,
Mikkel Eriksen, Nicholas Boundy, Christian Løchstøer
to be identified as the authors of this work has been asserted
by them in accordance with the Copyright, Designs and Patents Act, 1988
A CIP catalogue record for this book is available from the British Library upon request

HB ISBN: 978-1-4711- 2193-7
PB ISBN: 978-1-4711- 2194-4
eBook ISBN: 978-1-4711- 2195-1
Printed in Australia by McPhersons Printing Group
3 5 7 9 10 8 6 4 2

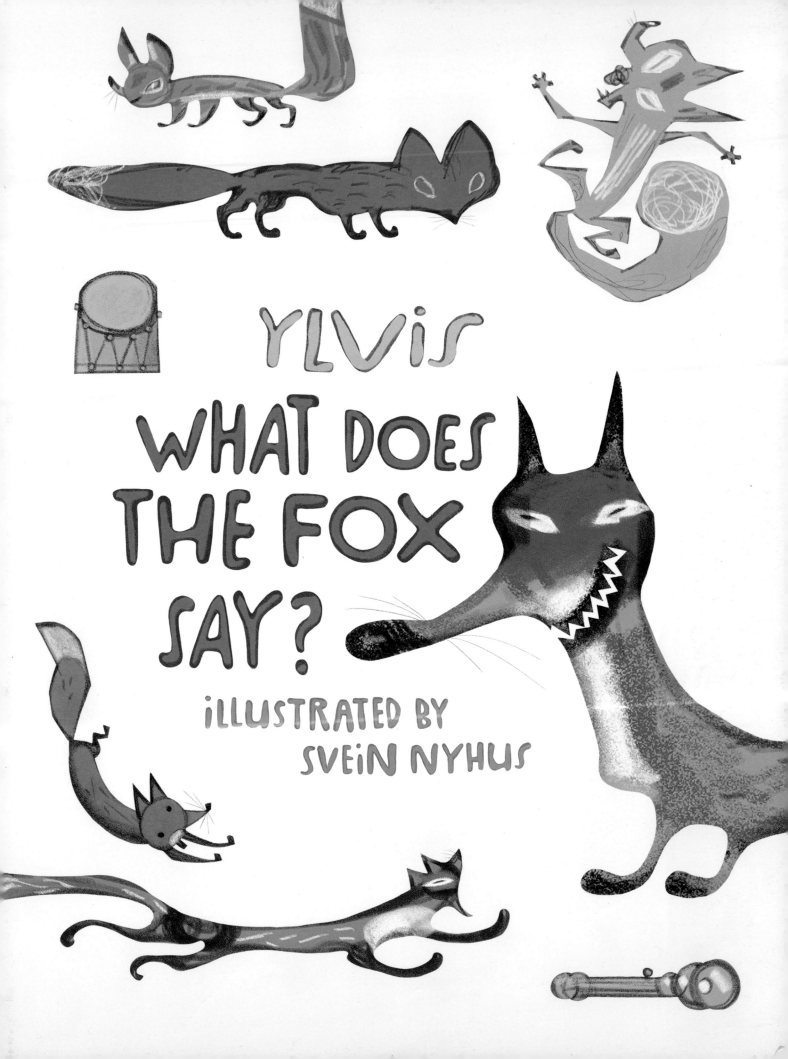

YLVIS
WHAT DOES THE FOX SAY?

ILLUSTRATED BY
SVEIN NYHUS

Dog goes woof

Cat goes meow

Bird goes tweet

and mouse goes squeak

Cow goes moo

Frog goes croak

and the elephant goes toot

Ducks say quack

and fish go blub

and the seal goes ow ow ow

But there is one sound

That no one knows

What does the fox say?

Ring-ding-ding-ding-
dingeringeding!
Gering-ding-ding-ding-
dingeringeding!
Ring-ding-ding-ding-
dingeringeding!

What does the fox say?

Wa-pa-pa-pa-pa-pa-pow!
Wa-pa-pa-pa-pa-pa-pow!
Wa-pa-pa-pa-pa-pa-pow!

What does the fox say?

Hatee-hatee-hatee-ho!

Hatee-hatee-hatee-ho!

Hatee-hatee-hatee-ho!

What does the fox say?

Joff-tchoff-tchoffo-tchoffo-tchoff!

Tchoff-tchoff-tchoffo-tchoffo-tchoff!

Joff-tchoff-tchoffo-tchoffo-tchoff!

What does the fox say?

Big blue eyes

Pointy nose

Chasing mice and digging holes

Tiny paws

Up the hill

Suddenly you're standing still

Your fur is red

So beautiful

Like an angel in disguise

But if you meet

a friendly horse

Will you communicate by morse?

How will you speak to that horse?

What does the fox say?

Jacha-chacha-chacha-chow!
Chacha-chacha-chacha-chow!
Jacha-chacha-chacha-chow!

What does the fox say?

Fraka-kaka-kaka-kaka-kow!
Fraka-kaka-kaka-kaka-kow!
Fraka-kaka-kaka-kaka-kow!

What does the fox say?

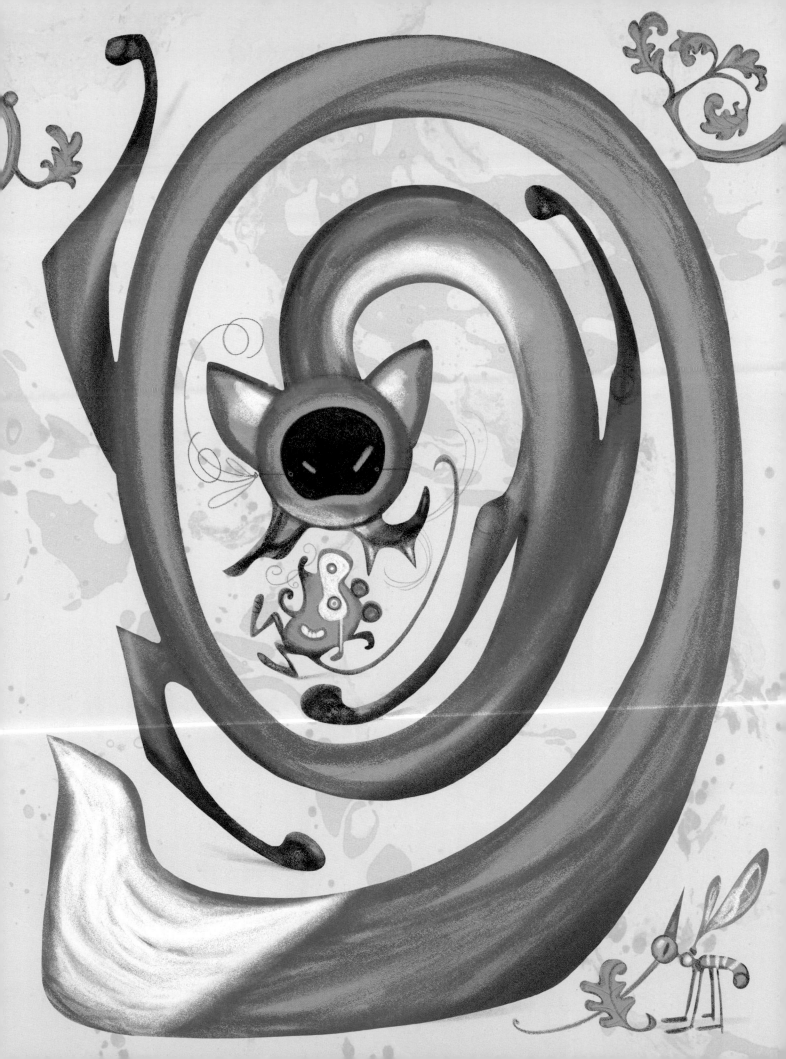

A-hee-ahee ha-hee!
A-hee-ahee ha-hee!
A-hee-ahee ha-hee!

What does the fox say?

A-oo-oo-oo-ooo!
Woo-oo-oo-ooo!

What does the fox say?

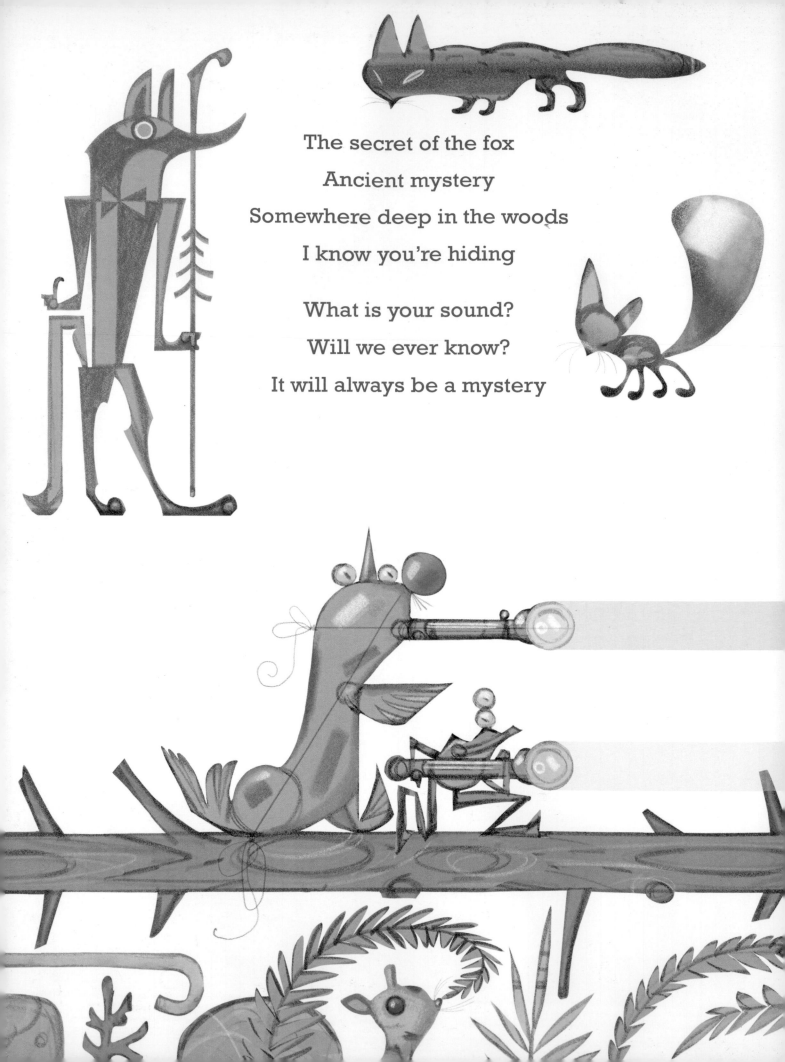

The secret of the fox

Ancient mystery

Somewhere deep in the woods

I know you're hiding

What is your sound?

Will we ever know?

It will always be a mystery

What do you say?
You're my guardian angel
Hiding in the woods
What is your sound?
Will we ever know?
I want to know!

Then, suddenly,
the fox said . . .

Boo-boo-bop-weydo
Boo-dee-bee-
beep-boo-beydo
Boo-boo-bop-weydo
Bee-bee-dee-
bap-bap-weydo
Ba-da-bap-beydo
bap-bap-weydo
Ba-da-bap-beydo!